For Dillon,
and for all those who see the world more deeply
—NF

To Pascal
—MA

Tundra Books, an imprint of Penguin Random House Canada Young Readers,
a Penguin Random House Company

Library and Archives Canada Cataloguing in Publication

Forler, Nan, author
Trampoline boy / by Nan Forler ; illustrated by Marion Arbona.

Issued in print and electronic formats.
ISBN 978-1-77049-830-3 (hardcover). — ISBN 978-1-77049-831-0 (EPUB)

I.Arbona, Marion, 1982-, illustrator II.Title.

PS8611.076T73 2018 jC813'.6 C2017-900513-8
C2017-900514-6

Published simultaneously in the United States of America by Tundra Books of
Northern New York, an imprint of Penguin Random House Canada Young Readers,
a Penguin Random House Company

Library of Congress Control Number: 2017930843

Edited by Tara Walker and Jessica Burgess
Designed by Andrew Roberts
The artwork in this book was rendered in gouache and pencil.
The text was set in Print Bold OT.

Printed and bound in China

www.penguinrandomhouse.ca

1   2   3   4   5   22   21   20   19   18

tundra   Penguin
Random House
TUNDRA BOOKS

TRAMPOLINE BOY

NAN FORLER & MARION ARBONA

tundra

Trampoline Boy liked to bounce.

Twirly-whirly,
loop-dee-loop.

Up he went
into the blue, blue sky.

In the sky, the boy gazed out
past
red wings on a blackbird,

BOING

above
airplanes drawing curly-cues,

BOING

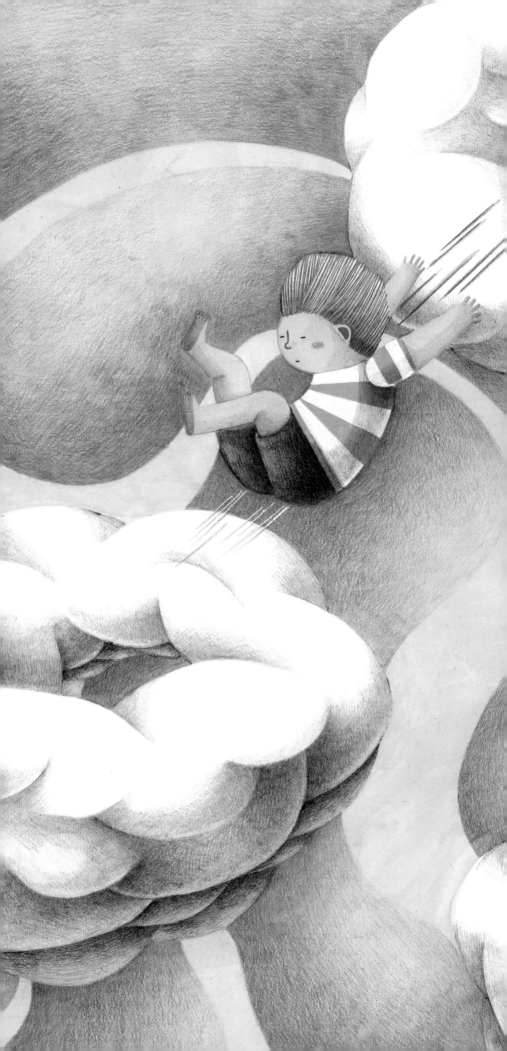

beyond
wispy, white clouds.

BOING

He bounced in the morning.

He bounced after school.

He bounced until the sky turned pink.

Kids called out as they passed,
"Hey, Trampoline Boy,
can't you do anything else?"

BOING

"What's the matter with you anyway?"

BOING

"Can't you hear?"

BOING

"He is so weird."

They'd scream and they'd shout,
but Trampoline Boy just kept bouncing,

as though
he hadn't heard.

The kids walked by,

but Peaches stopped.

She wriggled under the fence
and looked.

She stared up
and down
at the boy

and waited.

Twirly-whirly,
loop-dee-loop.

Up he went
into the blue, blue sky.

Every morning, Peaches crawled
under the fence.

Every afternoon,
she stood by the trampoline.

Every evening, she sat on the
dewy, green grass
and watched him bounce.

One day, Peaches,
in her teeniest, tiniest voice,
whispered,

"Trampoline Boy,
I wish I could see what you see
up there in that blue, blue sky."

BOI - 0I -

Trampoline Boy stopped bouncing.

He crawled off the trampoline
and stood beside Peaches,

then peered closely at her face.

They helped each other up,
and Peaches searched his eyes.

"Show me," she said.

Together
they started to bounce.

Twirly-whirly,
loop-dee-loop.

Up, up they went.

They gazed
way past
red wings on a blackbird

BOING BOING

to a place that was deep and bright,
high above
airplanes drawing curly-cues,

BOING BOING

where the world was
clear and true,

far beyond
wispy, white clouds

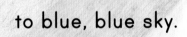

to blue, blue sky.